W9-BMQ-463

Oonga Boonga

To David and Suzie, who share something special

F. W.

For Clare and Chloë

C. T.

PUFFIN BOOKS
Published by the Penguin Group
Penguin Putnam Books for Young Readers,
345 Hudson Street, New York, New York, 10014, U.S.A.
Penguin Books Ltd., 27 Wrights Lane, London W8 5TZ, England
Penguin Books Australia Ltd., Ringwood, Victoria, Australia
Penguin Books Canada Ltd, 10 Alcorn Avenue, Toronto, Ontario, Canada M4V 3B2
Penguin Books (N.Z.) Ltd, 182-190 Wairau Road, Auckland 10, New Zealand

Penguin Books Ltd., Registered Offices: Harmondsworth, Middlesex, England

First Published in the United States of America by Dutton Children's Books,
a division of Penguin Putnam Books for Young Readers, 1999
Originally published in Great Britain by Transworld Publishers Ltd, London, 1998
Published by Puffin Books, a division of Penguin Putnam Books for Young Readers, 2001

3 5 7 9 10 8 6 4 2

Text copyright © Frieda Wishinsky, 1998
Illustrations copyright © Carol Thompson, 1998
All rights reserved

CIP Data is available.

Puffin Books ISBN 0-14-056840-9

Printed in Singapore

Except in the United States of America, this book is sold subject to the condition that it shall not by way of trade or otherwise be lent, re-sold, hired out, or otherwise circulated without the publisher's prior consent in any form of binding or cover other than that in which it is published and without a similar condition including this condition being imposed on the subsequent purchaser.

Oonga Boonga

Frieda Wishinsky • illustrated by Carol Thompson

PUFFIN BOOKS

Nobody could make

Baby Louise stop crying.

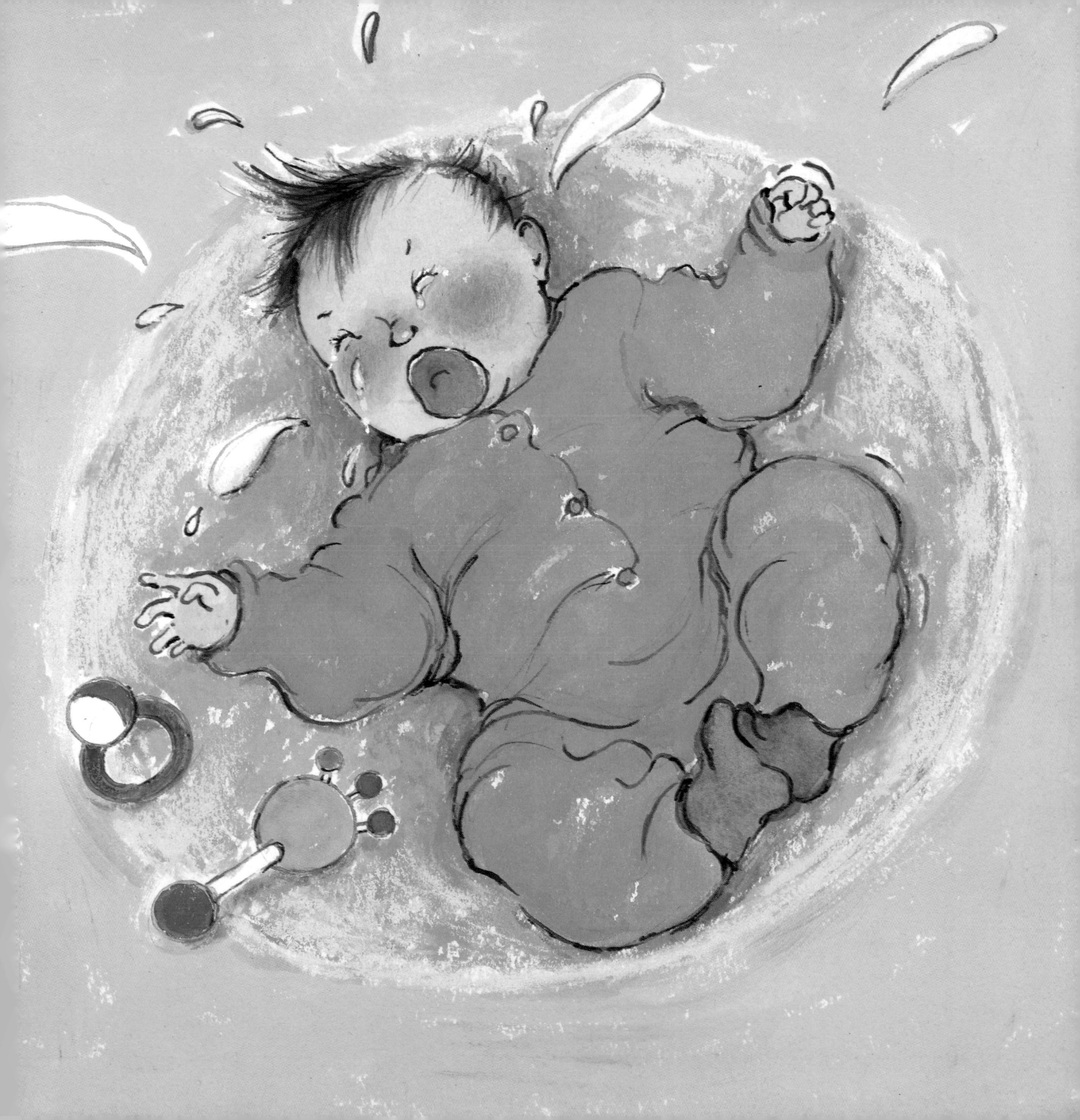

Her mother tried.

She held her close and sang a little lullaby.

But that didn't help.

Louise kept on crying until her tears ran

like rivers to the sea.

Her father tried.

He rocked her gently in his arms

and whispered softly in her ear.

But that didn't help.

Louise kept on crying until her wails

shook the pictures off the walls.

Grandma tried.

She gave her a nice warm bottle

and said, "Eat, eat."

But that didn't help.

Louise kept on crying until her sobs

woke all the dogs and cats on the block.

Grandpa tried.

He played a happy tune on his harmonica

and did a little jig.

But that didn't help.

Louise kept on crying till the birds flew out of the trees

and the squirrels scampered away.

The neighbors came and offered advice.

"Turn her on her stomach."

"Turn her on her side."

"Play Mozart."

"Play rock and roll."

But nothing helped. Louise kept on crying.

Then her brother, Daniel, came home from school.

"**Oonga boonga**," he said to Louise.

Louise looked up, tears streaming down her face.

"**Oonga boonga**," he repeated.

Louise stopped sobbing and looked him

straight in the eye.

"**Oonga boonga**," said Daniel again.

Louise broke into a smile.

"How did you do that?" asked his mother.

"It's easy. You just say **Oonga boonga**," said Daniel.

"Oonga boonga," said his mother.

"Oonga boonga," said his father.

"Oonga boonga," said Grandma and Grandpa.

"See," said Daniel. "She likes it."

And sure enough, she did.

Louise was smiling from ear to ear.

"Oonga boonga," said everyone in unison.

"I'm going out to play," said Daniel.

"Be back at six for dinner," said his mother.

But as soon as he left, Louise's smile faded.

Slowly a tear rolled down her cheek,

followed by another and then another.

And soon she was crying as loudly as before.

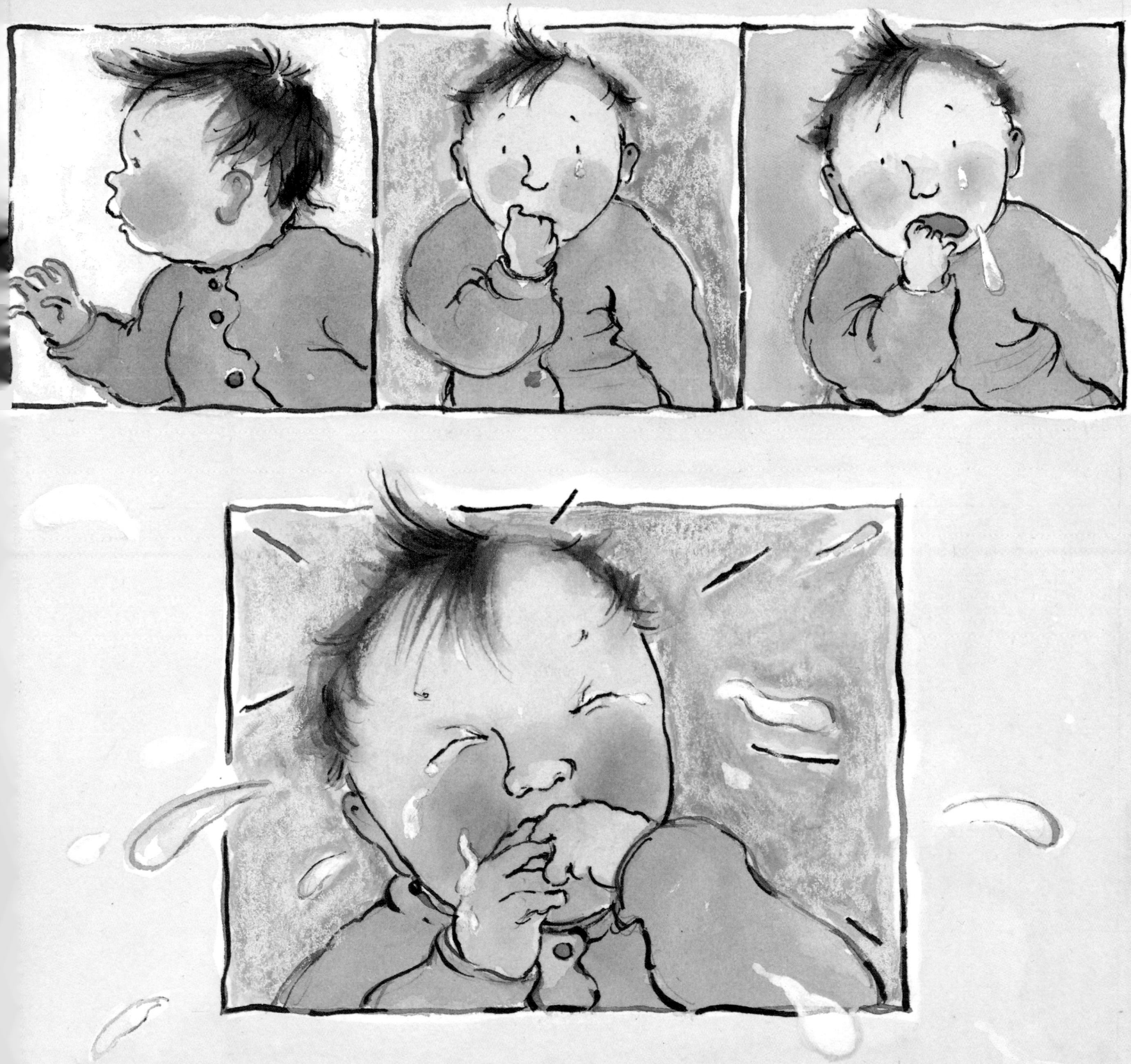

"Oonga boonga," said her mother.

"Oonga boonga," said her father.

"Oonga boonga," said Grandma and Grandpa.

But nothing helped. Louise kept on crying.

"What's wrong?" said Daniel.

"Oonga boonga doesn't work anymore," they said.

Wah
Wah
waah
agh!

Daniel leaned over Louise

and whispered in her ear:

"**Bunka wunka**, Louise."

And Louise stopped crying.